I0588411

THREE
TERRIBLE
TALES

by

MARGARET F.
CHEN

Printed through Opus Self-Publishing Services
Located at:
Politics and Prose Bookstore
5015 Connecticut Ave. NW
Washington, D.C. 20008
www.politics-prose.com / / (202) 364-1919

ACKNOWLEDGEMENTS

"Mephistopheles in Miami" by Margaret F. Chen. First published in *Rose Red Review*. Copyright © 2014 by Margaret F. Chen.

"The Pirate from Blackmoor" by Margaret F. Chen. First published in *Mulberry Fork Review*. Copyright © 2017 by Margaret F. Chen.

CONTENTS

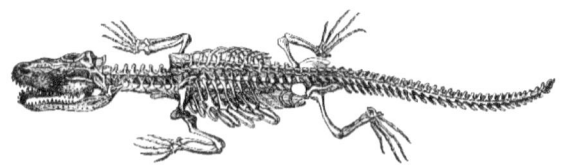

Mephistopheles in Miami

Someone is moving in upstairs. I know because I heard footsteps up there yesterday, thudding from one end of the apartment to the other. I was in my kitchen, preparing a lunch of lemonade and a grilled cheese sandwich, when I heard the footsteps, and I stopped and listened. They creaked through all the rooms above, pausing once in the master bedroom, and once in the kitchen—I know where the master bedroom and the kitchen are upstairs because my floor plan (the "Cambria") is exactly the same as the one above. Both apartments were vacant when I first called The Evergreen's leasing office two months ago, and I had chosen the lower unit; the upper one has remained empty, until now. I heard the kitchen window upstairs roll open upon its track, and then slide shut again, snapping back into its lock. The footsteps then stumped back across the living room, and down the outside staircase, which is located directly to the right of my front door. By the time I thought of abandoning my sandwich to look out the window, the stranger was gone. I peered through the half-closed slats of the vertical blinds, but all I could see were the waving shadows of the eucalyptus trees on the sidewalk. I watched and waited a few more moments, but whoever it was did not come back. This occurred on a Friday, and now it is Saturday afternoon. I am sitting at my cluttered dining-room table—a heavy, wooden, former library cast-off—drinking green tea in shadowy darkness (a disadvantage of these "garden units") while the cool, autumn sun lingers outside the patio door and slants down upon the fence enclosing the yard. A neighbor's air conditioner gives a low and steady hum, and children's voices rise and fall in the distance, echoing like far-away bells. Someone is singing, a melancholy, classical tune in a high, thin voice, probably a pale and willowy music student practicing for a concert. I have not heard the footsteps yet today, but of course, this new tenant probably won't be moving in right away. He or she must have been just checking the unit out yesterday; maybe he (or she) wanted to get an idea of where the furniture might go. I am both disappointed and excited by this turn of events. Disappointed because I will be losing the relative peace and quiet I had possessed, with an empty apartment upstairs, and myself on the ground floor in a corner unit. Excited because there will finally be a new person moving in, and perhaps we can be friends. Since moving to this apartment complex last month, I had been hoping to make friends, meet some of my neighbors, but I have found little in common with the young families that live here. Because it is summer, the children run about all day, to and from the swimming pool, up and down the paths, shouting at one another, and when they happen to be near my apartment when I venture out, they all stop their noisy activity as if on cue and stare at me.

I don't blame them. I do seem out of place here—an awkwardly tall, thin, unattached woman, with pinned-up dark-brown hair, always dressed in drab skirts, white blouses, flat shoes, and my floppy-brimmed, brown hat (they probably call me the "hat lady"). Someone who stays home all day, and doesn't "go to work." I can understand the children's (and their parents') curiosity. How do I make my living, for example? If any of them had asked, I would have answered that I was a freelance writer—but, of course, that's such a vague, unsatisfying answer. Most people—those who have the time, those who are curious, those who have asked in the past—usually want to know more. So, I go on to explain I specifically write biographies—on interesting and accomplished but obscure men and women. For example, my last project was a biography on the Art Deco painter, Sonya Lampiere; before that, I had completed a work on a rare-orchid breeder, named Marcus Thal. My focus for the past year has been on George Thomas Bethany, a creator and builder of roller coasters for various amusement parks along the East Coast. It is because of

George Bethany I am here, in this town—in this very apartment.

I had first seen a portrait of Bethany in a small university library, where I had been researching Marcus Thal. Both had grown up in Brooklyn where I lived before moving to the Florida, and both had graduated from the same school. I was immediately struck by Bethany's resemblance to a favorite cousin of mine, James, now living in London—the same whitish-blonde hair, thick eyebrows, light blue eyes, long, bony face, thin mouth, and high cheekbones. The uncanny resemblance sparked my initial interest in Bethany as my next subject. And when I found out more about Bethany, I was hooked.

George Bethany was an American inventor and businessman born in the mid-1800s, an innovator of roller-coaster design; he modeled his "gravity" railways after the coal mining cars of eastern Pennsylvania, and went on to build several of the first commercially successful roller-coasters on the East Coast, and a few in Florida and Chicago. Besides inventing the modern roller-coaster, he also conceived of the idea of having paying customers for his "pleasure rides"—thus opening up an entire new industry of amusement parks. After becoming extremely wealthy, George had retired at the age of fifty to this town outside of Miami. Two of his descendants, Michael Bethany and John Dorset, had started a real estate business, eventually building several hotels and apartment complexes throughout Florida, North Carolina, Virginia, and Texas. I had already spoken to John Dorset over the phone, and would be meeting with him and his brother sometime next month. Michael was currently on business overseas, and John was visiting family in Virginia. The Evergreen, the apartment complex I had chosen, was a resort-style assemblage of cottages, several two-story buildings, and one sprawling, castle-like, central building. It was built in the 1950s and very conveniently located, close to the city library, restaurants, and Bethany's former home. Here I intended to stay—for as long as I needed to.

There were many pleasant surprises when I had first moved in, such as the spaciousness of the private backyards, the luxuriant flowers and trees. My garden was bare when I arrived, as I had requested—only a small patio and a smooth, dirt ground, ready for planting. So far, I have installed only a few rose bushes and a lemon tree, some pots of daylilies and daisies. The neighbors on my left seem not to have done much with their yard, either; I can see long patches of bare ground through the slats of the fence separating us; a rusty bike leans against the stucco wall near their patio door, and bright, plastic toys are scattered about. Sometimes I see someone watering a potted plant hanging outside the patio door. I always call out hello, if we both happen to be outside at the same time, although I am not sure exactly with whom I am speaking.

Although I don't know these neighbors well, they are

friendly, and we always say hello to each other. I think they are Vietnamese or Korean (I sometimes accidentally get their mail, addressed to a Rosalyn or Jin Park)—a mom, a dad, a grandmother, and two young children. Sometimes aunts and uncles or friends visit. An assortment of shoes—green and yellow and pink striped slippers, tiny red flats, brown loafers—sit in rows on the welcome mat, neatly lining their front entrance. Once I caught a glimpse of the family, through their open front door, sitting around the table, eating their dinner. A strong, delicious, tangy smell drifted out upon the summer breeze—limes and coconut, I think. I went back to my own apartment, and looked up various Vietnamese noodle soup recipes on the internet, but the directions sounded terribly complicated, so I cut up some vegetables and made a ratatouille instead. Anyway, I like the family next door, and the other families I see around the complex, and I like the front office staff. But I never move beyond the standard small talk with any of them. They all seem so self-contained, so politely uninterested. And unfortunately, there has been a complete turnover of all three leasing agents and the manager since I moved in. I had just gotten on friendly terms with the old manager and the assistants when one by one, they all vanished, to be replaced by at first one and then two, tall blonde, stylish women managers.

Over the rest of the week, between organizing new information about George Bethany retrieved from the

Museum of Southeastern Florida's archives, and typing up
the chapter on his mysterious illness and death at the age of
fifty-two, I continue to try and catch a glimpse of the new
tenant. But every time I hear footsteps outside on the
staircase, and look through the peephole in my front door,
I only see the distorted backs of the moving men or the
elongated figures of one of the two tall blonde apartment
managers. Where was the tenant? One time I catch a
glimpse of a shorter woman, with cropped dark hair, and
excitedly think, "She must be the one." But I see her again,
later, just as I am coming home from getting groceries,
walking beside a tall, balding man in khaki shorts and a
brown-and-gray striped polo shirt. They do not seem to
match each other—he is dressed like a middle-management
type in his weekend clothes, and she in a bright yellow
pantsuit. I hear the man say, "...and then she passed away
last summer." It is in the hopeful tone of a lonely man out
on a first date, trying too hard, telling too much too soon,
things that are too private. I figure out, from this
conversation, that the man and the short-haired woman are
not together—she is in all likelihood a new leasing assistant
whom I have not yet met, merely showing the upstairs
apartment to a prospect. Yet, only a few days ago I had
watched men in white shirts and black shorts, a sort of
moving company uniform, I think, hauling a queen-size
mattress and a mirrored dresser up the stairs. They had
moved other things up too but I quit watching after the bed

and the dresser. I was sure I would see the new tenants that very evening, when I picked up my mail by the front office. But no one ever did appear.

On Sunday, I take a break from the illness and death chapters. I think these chapters are beginning to get to me—last night I dreamed I was floating in an abandoned swimming pool, one full of old rainwater and draining slowly; greenish moss covered the grayish, stone walls of the pool. I am never very hungry in the mornings, but today, after the dream, the bland brown toast and tea look even more unappetizing than usual. The Sunday paper sits on the table, with its black headlines and smeary photos. I feel tired and dull and can't bring myself to pick up the inky paper, not even flip to the book reviews or the Style section for a jolt of entertainment. Instead, I put on one of my father's records—Frankie Valli and the Four Seasons—and sit and stare at the mass of photos and collection of magnets covering my refrigerator—souvenirs from amusement parks, cities, and state parks; magnets shaped like leaves and cans of soda or chocolate bars, or resembling old-fashioned signs or comic books or replicas of famous paintings. I am very fond of my magnets, each one collected at a different place and time. My favorite magnet is a black and white, 1950s photo of a man and woman—husband and wife, boyfriend and girlfriend, I assume—riding a roller coaster, laughing and bravely waving their hands in the air as they plunge down the five-hundred foot track; "The Inferno:

Coney Island!" is printed in a curly, circus-script above their smiling faces. The Inferno was one of George Bethany's roller-coasters. I think of how ironic the name, The Inferno, is—George Bethany himself had been a devout man and former Sunday school teacher. There is a sense of defiance in it all, though. The man and woman laugh and seem to say: See? We're flying down The Inferno—it's fun! I may love my magnets more, I'm afraid, than the photos they frame and surround on the refrigerator. There are photos of me, at different ages; photos of old school friends and old boyfriends. There is one of James, wearing a fedora and smoking a cigar; I confess, I had a crush on James as a teenager, although he is now married, to a childhood classmate, named Therese. I hear from James and Therese occasionally—a Christmas card, a birthday card, a phone call when someone is in town and wants to drop in for a visit.

There are also photos of my parents. My father had taken hundreds of pictures of our little family before he died. I don't remember anything about my father, and I was never close to my mother (she fell apart after my father's death and ceased paying much attention to me—you could say I mostly brought up myself). Most of the photos seem surreal to me—they have, in fact, taken on the insistently happy yet impersonal frozen aura of a magazine ad or a stranger's family photos. Or maybe they more resemble the patient photos crammed onto the bulletin board at my dentist's office—pictures of smiling strangers, engaged energetically in activities I know nothing about. I have mulled over many of my refrigerator photos, and it seems they could be interchangeable with the ones at my dentist's office. I don't know that toddler girl with the curly hair in the yellow dress, holding onto her father's hand, frowning into the camera, or sitting in a field of daisies, laughing in her mother's arms—this must be another child. Yet, she looks like me.

That evening, dozing in front of the news, with photos of George Bethany and his roller-coasters on the coffee table, waiting to be sorted, I hear something upstairs, a bumping noise. It must be my new neighbor, as it is Sunday, and there wouldn't be any of the office staff working now. There is the sound of the tap being turned on in the bathroom—the water rushes on and on, like a waterfall muffled behind a cave wall, and I assume that someone is taking a bath. Then the tap squeaks shut; there is singing, a scratchy tenor voice, in a foreign language, as from a recording—not quite opera, definitely not something contemporary. Who would listen to such music in the bathtub? I imagine a woman, with aromatic candles set up all around the darkened room. Yet, the footsteps that creak on my ceiling, after a while, sound heavy, like a man's. The television above turns on—the news, just like on my own television. My watch says six o'clock—it isn't too late. I can go upstairs, make up some excuse to meet this new person.

There is no one outside, and even the birds are silent; the waning sun has disappeared behind a bank of gray clouds, and the wind waves the slender trees back and forth. I peer up at the outside staircase and see lights seeping through the window blinds in the upstairs apartment. I run up and knock on the door; there is no answer, although I can hear the television. I knock again. It finally occurs to me this person is not going to ever appear. Or at the very least, I don't think he or she can hear me. I climb back down the stairs, and go back into my apartment. A thudding noise from outside my patio door terrifies me; at first, I am rooted to the carpeted floor. But then I run towards the sound, slide open the glass patio door, and step outside. I am in my fenced-in, dusty garden—the sun edges out from behind the fast-moving clouds, and late sunlight illuminates the yard once more. The six-foot privacy fence has a door which I rarely use, leading out to the parking lot and down past the walled-in backyards of single-family homes, and I see that this fence door is slightly ajar. But, if someone had been here—wouldn't there be footprints in the dirt, leading towards the door? There aren't any. I peek out around the gate before latching it again—there is a shadow walking away, sauntering down the sidewalk past the houses of the neighborhood. It is a very tall, thin shadow—that of a man's, wearing a blazer and pair of loose light-colored trousers. I can't tell the exact shade of his clothes or even his hair because he is too far away, whether due to evening shadows or their natural color. The man seems to be enjoying the sunset, not in any hurry at all. He picks off a flower from a tree hanging over a wall from someone's backyard, tucks it into his shirt pocket, and continues down the street.

The television upstairs chatters all night, keeping me awake, and in the morning, I feel dazed from lack of sleep. I call the new maintenance man—Albert, a tanned, barrel-shaped person with two dark-brown commas for a mustache—who arrives at nine, and allows me to go upstairs with him to see what is going on. He knocks on the door, and unlocks it, when there is no answer. The light is still on in the living room, and just as I have insisted to Albert all along, the television is talking away.

"Well," says Albert. "That's really strange."

"Strange? Why?" I ask. "Who lives here now?"

"No one," he says. "This is a model unit."

I look around, and sure enough the furniture is all immaculate and perfect, in a generic sort of way—an olive-colored upholstered sofa set; the cream and brown square-patterned rug; the matching glass coffee and end tables; the white wood dining set.

"But," I say," why did you knock if you knew this was a model unit?"

Albert shrugs. "I don't know. I mean, with you telling me about the television and all. Maybe there was someone living here. The office doesn't always tell me everything."

"I heard someone here last night," I say. "Taking a bath." I hurry into the bathroom, but everything is in dark and perfect order—the fluffy brown bath mat; the dry, folded towels; the unused bar of soap by the sink.

Albert says, "It doesn't look like anyone was here. Maybe you heard a different neighbor?"

A model apartment—of course, that explains everything. I am relieved the mystery is over. Yet there is a nagging feeling, a lot of things don't quite fit; I resolve to call the front office later to hear what they have to say about Albert's report; I want this straightened out, once and for all. It is obvious to me the leasing staff doesn't communicate well with either tenants or maintenance. Not only is there never any notice when the old staff leaves and new people start, now Albert is confessing the office doesn't always tell him what is going on, either. If the upstairs apartment is a model unit, for example, who has been using it? Why doesn't Albert know who it is? Someone had been taking a bath, watching television, for godsakes. Why isn't he more interested or concerned? Was it that man I saw behind the parking lots? Was it even safe here? That man could have been in my backyard, although I am beginning to question whether I had really heard a thud outside my patio door yesterday. I find myself going over different scenarios— maybe someone is about to move in and Albert doesn't know it yet, maybe someone is sneaking in—that tall, thin man!—and using the apartment, maybe someone has already rented the unit—one of the leasing agents, for example—and that man was the boyfriend. These are the only explanations I can think of at the moment. But I can't focus on the problem anymore, as my editor calls and wants to know where my next George Bethany chapters are; I draw the blinds in my bedroom, sit at my cramped desk, and try to work.

By noon I have sifted through all the published material surrounding Bethany's death—family testimonials, autopsy reports (death by drowning), health records, newspaper, magazine articles—and start writing. I also have plenty of my own material to work with, having conducted several interviews last year with various, scattered descendants— some were still living in Brooklyn, some in the Midwest, a great grandson and his wife and their grandchildren were out in Southern California. There is something really off about George Bethany's death—how could someone who was once a high-school swimming champion just drown on a boating trip taken on a calm, clear-skied day? This mystery preoccupies me so thoroughly, I forget about calling the apartment office about the upstairs mystery. When I finally remember to do this, at around three in the afternoon, the line is busy. It is past five when I think about walking to the office in person; I decide to go there first thing in the morning.

I am searching in my refrigerator for something to make for dinner, when I hear shuffling noises upstairs again. Just like yesterday, the tap in the bathroom turns on. I hear the same music, and then, again, footsteps to the living room. I hurry outside and up the staircase, remembering too late that I have no shoes on, and my hair and clothes are awry.

The front door to the apartment is open. Someone says, "Come in." Where have I heard that voice before? I know it—a smooth, lilting voice, with a hint of laughter just beneath the surface. If I had a favorite kind of voice, that would be it. Sitting at the white dining table is the tall, thin man I saw yesterday, strolling down the sidewalk—or, I think it is the same man. There is a lavender vase of purple and white orchids (which was not there yesterday) and two porcelain cups of tea (somehow, I know it is tea) arranged precisely on the table. As for the person sitting in front of me, there is something very familiar about him. His longish hair is not dark, as I imagined last night, but very blond, almost white in color, as are his long eyelashes and thick eyebrows. His eyes are such a light blue, they look almost colorless, and his face is angular, with a high forehead and cheekbones. He is very pale, and dressed rather formally and very warmly for an August afternoon—a tweed blazer, pressed trousers, an oxford shirt, polished loafers. This man—he is not handsome, although individually, his features are quite good.

This man looks somewhat familiar.

He looks like my cousin, James.

No—like George Bethany.

Like both, or either.

I realize I am flustered and out of breath—from nervousness, from shock. Instead of moving backwards, however—carefully back out the door and down the stairs—I walk forward.

"Amanda Genevieve Langdon," he says. "Greetings."

"How did you know my name?"

"I overheard," he says. "Somewhere."

From Albert, I thought. But I wondered when Albert had ever called me by my full name. "You live here then?"

"Yes."

"But I was told this was a model unit."

He laughs, and his pale eyes suddenly seemed to take on a warmer, deeper color for a moment, but maybe I just imagine that.

I persist (rather rudely, I admit), "Where are you from? Was that you I heard up here yesterday?"

"Probably," he says. "I'm sorry—was I being loud?"

Here I flush a little, as I know I speak rather loudly myself sometimes, when I am on the phone. What had he heard?

The man continues slyly, "Would you like some tea?" He nods towards the cups on the table. I wonder how he knew I would be coming. It is just a coincidence, I tell myself. He might have tea every afternoon at this time. The extra cup is for any visitors who might drop by. When he sees my hesitation, he says, jokingly, "Don't be afraid. It's just tea. I promise."

I step up to the table, and suddenly poke him in the arm. He does not look surprised, and I am not surprised he isn't surprised.

"You're real," I say.

"Of course."

"Who are you?"

"But I've told you. I'm your neighbor."

"You look like my cousin, James," I say. "A little."

The man smiles, "That, I think, is a compliment. But I am not James—my name is Richard." He takes a long sip of tea, and then clears his throat, as if he is about to give a lecture. "You've been working too hard, Amanda. All that work and where does it get you? No friends, no family, a one-bedroom apartment, here in…*The Evergreen*—," here he makes an exaggerated flourish with his right arm and rolls his eyes. "And so, here I am. To help you. I know what you've been up to. Your search to understand certain persons—difficult, elusive persons, I know. 'Those who know her know her less—the nearer they get.' Or maybe I should say 'him'? Who said that, by the way?"

"Emily Dickinson."

"Yes. Emily." The man says this as if he knows her, and I laugh out loud at his ridiculousness. He laughs, too, good-naturedly. He has beautiful, white teeth, which, again, doesn't surprise me at all.

"You've chosen some interesting people, haven't you," he says.

"What do you mean?"

"Well, there's George Bethany. You find it unbelievable he was murdered, don't you? That people whose business it is to amuse others would end up that way. And George was such a generous, kind-hearted man."

I am shocked into a long silence. The abandoned swimming pool from my dreams forms itself again in my mind—I had read about Bethany's death by drowning over and over again in the papers. All accounts had insisted he had fallen off his boat, while sailing with his wife and another couple, their best friends.

I say, "It was an accident. I checked every single article and interview. The hospital and death records. All of them confirm it was an accident." But I know what Richard says is true. It had occurred to me, despite all the "official" reports I had read in my research. Bethany had been hiding out in southeastern Florida. Who would believe roller coaster inventors had any enemies?

"That's what I like about you, Amanda. You do a good job."

"What do you mean?" I say. "How do you know what I do?" I back away, torn between wanting to continue my conversation with this Richard, and thinking I should call the police as soon as I get back downstairs. Of course, I am not sure for what reason I would need to call the police.

Richard wasn't really doing anything wrong. In fact, he had nicely invited me for tea. But also, he might be some kind of lunatic or stalker, although he looked charming and normal. I didn't know what to do. *Just get downstairs*, I tell myself. *Pretend you aren't scared.*

Richard laughs again—an open, innocent, almost boisterous laugh. He begins to hum something familiar. I have the urge to laugh, too, and suddenly, I relax a bit.

"This is all a joke," I say, maybe more to myself than Richard. "I wanted someone to talk to, I needed someone—and so you came, is that it? Someone sent you. Who sent you?"

"No one sent me, Amanda," Richard says patiently. "I'm sorry if I alarmed you. Let me assure you—I am your friend. Your neighbor. That's all you need to know. Hey, you're tired. So good night—for now. Come back later—tomorrow maybe. We'll talk about your work. George Bethany. Anything you like. Whatever is on your mind."

The door, I notice now, is open—had it been like that, the entire time? Had anyone else seen? I hurry down the stairs without looking back at Richard, but a sensation of dizziness hits me, and I sit down on the bottom step, and lean my head against the handrail. Everything becomes a little blurry, and I try to focus on the neat row of shoes lined up in front of the Parks' door. They remind me of my own feet, bare and cold—I have the overwhelming urge to slip my feet into a pair of those shoes. The fluffy slippers look comfortable and warm. I notice that the father's loafers are missing, which means he probably hasn't come home from work yet. The mother's red slippers are also missing. But strangely, I see them—the missing red slippers—coming towards me on the sidewalk—with Mrs. Park's white-socked feet in them. The sequins on the shoes sparkle in the waning sunlight. I squint up at her; she is carrying the mail.

"Miss Amanda?" Mrs. Park's high, tiny voice floats down. "Are you okay?"

After a minute or two, I tell her a little too sharply I am fine, although I can't seem to lift my head from the iron handrails.

"You don't look okay." Mrs. Parks hauls me up—she's surprisingly strong, tiny as she is—and I lean on her soft, sweatered arm. I sneak a look up at the upstairs apartment, but the door is closed and the window is dark.

"Mrs. Park," I say suddenly, pointing upstairs. "Do you know who the new tenant is there?"

"No new tenant," she says, with raised eyebrows. "That Mr. Richard Bethany. He stays here sometimes. But he used to be in another apartment. Over there," she waves vaguely in the opposite direction, towards the pool and main office. "His family owns complex. And others, too." I shudder a little, but it makes sense. Of course. Richard Bethany— Michael Bethany's son? He was supposed to be traveling with his father. But instead, here he is, and I don't know why. And moving into the apartment above mine was definitely not a coincidence. Richard said he was here to help, after all. Now I will be able to find out what really happened to George Bethany. I can set the record straight about his death. And Richard, his descendent, this terribly handsome man—someone who looks like my cousin, James, no less—is here to help me with my latest, my most fascinating—and perhaps my last—biography.

What more could I have asked for?

The sweet smell of orange blossoms is so overpowering I become unsteady and almost fall again. I had never noticed such a heavy concentration of the flowers by the stairs before. Mrs. Park feels me swaying and grabs hold of my arm even tighter.

So, I know I'll be going up to see my friend, Richard, again soon. But for now, Mrs. Park and I walk together, stumble rather, towards her warm, good-smelling apartment. I know I'll be safe there, even if it is for just a little while.

The Pirate from Blackmoor

It is noon on Friday, and I am assembling the last hundred brochures for the upcoming Third Annual Elementary Educators Conference, when Jennifer Elroy, my supervisor, strides in from the conference room next door. Close upon her heels is Lowell Schumacher, a pale, lanky science-education writer and her co-worker. I think he and Jennifer are dating, although Jennifer won't admit it. She says they are just friends.

"Sarah. Just the person I wanted to see," says Jennifer. "Could you enter these into the database today? Thanks so much, dear." She places a stack of journals on my desk, pages marked with bright pink and lime-green sticky-notes—the array of colored notes look like the blunted feathers of some kind of girl-power headdress.

I say, okay, but stifle a sigh. Not only was I hoping to leave on time today, which will now be impossible, I am expecting someone important very soon, and want to have the office all to myself when he comes by. But Jennifer continues to stand at my desk, flipping through the mail, while Lowell, hands in pockets, rocks gently back and forth on his heels, pretending not to mind Jennifer's noisy mail-flipping. I say to Jennifer, thinking she would want to know, "Ruth asked me to finish mailing out these brochures this afternoon. Is it okay if I finish up the journals on Monday? I don't think I'll be able to get Ruth's mailing done if I stop now." Ruth Bowman is the Bowman Foundation's senior director, and Jennifer's and Lowell's supervisor. After a brief and possibly calculated pause, Jennifer looks up from the mail. Her wide mouth stretches up at the sides, revealing large, perfect white teeth, but her depthless-black, close-set eyes are cold and studying.

"Oh. Of course," she says. "Monday will be fine." I recoil a little—there is something in her voice I can't quite place. Maybe she thinks I'm trying to put her off. And I'm not, I remind myself. I really do have to get the brochures out. Then I notice Lowell watching me closely, too, and I wonder if I've said something that has embarrassed Jennifer, whom he adores, or at least, follows around. But Jennifer doesn't look embarrassed. I tell myself not to be so paranoid. I haven't done anything wrong. There are no grant deadlines for another three months, and entering journal information into the database, used only for creating bibliographies for Jennifer's articles, is the least important of my jobs. Still, I feel anxious about Jennifer's chilly response, and I wonder if I should ask if there is anything the matter. But it's unlikely that she'll enlighten me, so I try not to worry about it further.

"Thank you," I say, and straighten the journals, which have spread out of their stacked pile all over my desk. Jennifer continues sorting through the mail, removing her own letters and journals; she asks, how was my spring vacation ("Quiet."), and how did I like my new place ("It's small, but convenient."), and what about Southern California itself ("The beach is great."). Jennifer has been extra kind to me after my grandmother—my guardian since the age of five—died last year. She offered to give me a few days off, which I accepted gratefully. My grandmother had left me a small inheritance, which if I was careful would last a long time. I could have probably taken more time off, but I preferred, after the funeral, to keep my life as normal as possible. As normal as it could have been, that is, without my grandmother, and only Cinema, my cat, to keep me company.

After picking up where I had left off with Ruth's brochure, I begin to breathe easier, telling myself that Jennifer's friendly questions indicate she isn't mad at me after all. She and Lowell have left my desk by now and are by the doorway laughing loudly together over a letter she has just opened. As usual, when I look at her, I am fascinated by her smooth, shiny, helmet of dark-brown hair; her slanted bangs are combed carefully off her brow at a perfect forty-five degree angle. I wonder how she is able to spray every strand down flat like that. Not a rebellious wisp dangles out of place. I wish my own hair could look like that. I notice that she is wearing black pants and a pink sweater today, a departure from her usual suits and collared shirts, and I admire how neat and authoritative she still looks, even while wearing such a pink sweater. She's softening her look, I conclude, she wants to come across as more feminine. At thirty-two, Jennifer is only two years older than I am, and three years older than Lowell (who matches her today, with his blue shirt, pink, discreetly diamond-patterned tie, and dark-gray pants), but she seems much more mature and self-assured than anyone else I know. She's also clever, successful, has a Bachelor's in Education, and was already a respected teacher-trainer before joining the Bowman Foundation's small group of education researchers two years ago. Whereas I am just an office assistant with a high-school diploma. It's true I'm attending night school—majoring in Art History—but that is turning out to be a struggle. I wish, as I sometimes do, that I could be a little more like Jennifer—confident, tactful, poised. She isn't beautiful, I acknowledge, or even pretty, but she has an aura of self-possession that is attractive, or at least convincing. She is also tall—what people might call "stately." Lowell is tall, too. They are like two tall trees. Standing beside them, taking back the filtered stack of mail, I am aware that they loom over me without much effort, and I probably resemble a child or dwarf. It shouldn't matter, probably, since I am practically invisible; plus, my skirt and blouse are horribly wrinkled today, and my hair has fallen down already from its once-elegant up-do. But I still fuss and worry over these details, because Ben will be here today—the very important person I am waiting for.

At twelve-thirty, every Friday, Ruth Bowman's son, Ben, who is a law student at Pomona University, drops by to have lunch with his mother. They go across the street for tapas at the Café Rafaela—spiced clams, shrimp croquettes, stuffed tomatoes. I know because he always tells me what they eat when they get back. He says it is his favorite restaurant, and once confessed, rather hesitantly, that he might even like to work there as a chef, or manager "because it might be fun." I was a little surprised, but pleased he would share this bit of information with me. I had thought about what he said for some time, and then concluded being a restaurant manager might be a better fit for him than law school. I've only seen Ben as friendly and easygoing, but never argumentative. But then again, I don't know many lawyers personally; maybe I have the wrong idea about them. Ben is still young—twenty-two—and wonderfully handsome. When he first started working here, a few months ago, I asked Jennifer who he was, and she had told me that he was Ruth's son.

"He's cute," I blurted, and she had laughed. "Yes, he's charming. And very intelligent."

"Is he single?"

"As far as I know."

She probably saw the plans spinning in my head, for she added quickly,"But I think he's transferring to New York University next year."

But Ben did not transfer. He continued to show up on Fridays, and for a time, we never said more than "Hello" to each other, or an occasional "How are you." But I had felt, just the tiniest bit he might've noticed and even liked me a little.

Sometime after my conversation with Jennifer, I had asked her again for her opinion—what did she think if I asked Ben out for coffee, and how did she think Ruth would feel about it?

"I don't think it would be a good idea," Jennifer stated.

"I could just try."

"I wouldn't recommend it."

I thought, Jennifer's just concerned I'll be upset if he says no or leaves town, for another school, and I felt glad she wanted to warn me.

"Okay," I said."Thanks for talking with me about it."

After that, Jennifer refused to hold any more discussions about Ben, although she continued to be politely interested in my life outside of work. I spoke to her about my art classes and about my grandmother, who used to take me to the art galleries and exhibits in the city. But although I tried to draw her out, Jennifer shared very little about her own life and background. I knew she had grown up in New York, state and that she had a wide network of friends and family still there—this is, at least, what she told me. Once or twice a year she took a short trip to visit everyone, and I was impressed, when she commented upon her exhausting social calendar. I regretted having asked her about Ben, because it had made her so uncomfortable. She probably just hadn't wanted to say anything bad about her boss's son. But she's wrong about Ben, I thought, and it wouldn't hurt for me to be friends with him.

Ben, then, is probably one of the reasons I have stayed at this job for so long. I'm pretty good at doing what I do (general office duties) and I could have at least gone someplace else that has windows. But I admit I may have also grown somewhat attached to the four, blank white walls surrounding my desk, the indestructible metal-colored carpet, the wood-veneer bookshelves and the fake plants, the fluorescent lighting which gives everyone an unearthly, bluish glow. I'm comfortable with my desk and computer and expensive, ergonomic chair, my calendar, the copier, the postage machine, and the two upholstered, burgundy-colored office chairs near my desk, provided for visitors. We are on the fourteenth floor of a brick building, and no one ever, ever visits, except the mailman, the delivery guy, the copier-toner guy, the water-cooler guy, and Ben, Ruth's son.

He is right on time today. When the door opens, I don't look up from my brochure-folding, but catch anyway, a blur of white shirt and jeans.

"Hi!" says Ben, and I answer, "Hi!"

Unfortunately, he is not talking to me, but to Jennifer and Lowell.

Lowell says, "Hey, Ben", and Jennifer says, "Hi, Ben. How's school going?"

Ben says something, but I'm too busy hiding behind my computer to pay attention to what it is. I'm startled when he suddenly appears by my desk.

"I see they're overworking you again," he says, looking down at the piles of yellow brochures, the stacks of mail, and Jennifer's journals. I turn red, am rendered speechless.

Jennifer saves me by interjecting, "I don't know what we'd do without Sarah." But she then changes the subject, and informs me about a luncheon she and Lowell will be attending that day, and how she won't be back until three-thirty. I am distracted by Ben, who is looking with serious attention at a book on my desk.

Jennifer instructs me to make extra copies of her "Managing Science Educators" paper, and then she and Lowell leave, for which I am not ungrateful.

"Sonya Lampiere!" Ben says. "Is this your book? You like her?"

"Yes. Yes, I do," I finally manage. The book is not entirely a coincidence. I know Ben loves Art Deco (a bit of information I had culled from Jennifer), and would know about Sonya Lampiere, a famous Art Deco painter from the 1930s. Sure enough, Ben waxes on about Lampiere's "Solitude" portraits, a series featuring famous writers and artists of the time, alone in their homes and studios, or in quiet, outdoor settings. I only hear about every other word Ben says; it is very pleasant just to look at him. He is casual about his dress and wears jeans, but he always manages to look stylish. So far this year, I don't think I've seen him wear the same shirt twice. Today he wears my new favorite—a white, short-sleeved, collared shirt, with tiny, colored flowers. I look closely at the small flowers—raspberry-colored, orange, violet, fuchsia, yellow, all with delicate, green stems. It is a beautiful and happy shirt.

"The Bechinger Art Museum," Ben is saying, "has some of her paintings on exhibit. Have you seen them yet?"

"No. But I hear it will be around until this summer." There is a hopeful note in my voice that he misses.

"You should go," he says. There is a long silence. This is the perfect time, I realize, to ask him if he'd like to see the Exhibit with me.

"Where did you get that shirt?" I ask. "I really like it."

"This? I don't remember. Macy's, maybe."

"It's very nice," I say. "Um. Do you want me to call your mom?" I was about to press her number on the intercom, but Ben shakes his head. "No, I'll just go back. Thanks."

He is about to go, but hesitates and turns back to smile at me. "See you around." It is more of a question than a statement. A good sign, I think. There is always next week. I take one last look at him, and try to file away, until then, the clear, blue color of his eyes, his generous smile, the coppery-smooth skin, the exact tone of his voice, the unhurried, graceful saunter of someone walking, not down a silent, windowless, fluorescent hallway, but outside, enjoying the afternoon sunshine.

The ticking of the clock hanging on the wall adjacent to my desk reminds me of how late it is, and when I look over, it indifferently tells me it is past six-thirty. There is no natural light to indicate the waning day, so it always looks the same in here, like the inside of a box. I listen to the ticking, and realize everyone has already left. The office had been unusually busy this afternoon, with the researchers seemingly passing back and forth in front of my desk endlessly, going in and out of the office—I think it's probably because of the conference coming up. There was one flurry of excitement, late in the afternoon, when Jennifer saw a spider on the wall, and ordered Lowell to kill it—which he did, grinning afterwards and looking rather pleased. I was a bit abashed at my unfeminine curiosity at the spider (I had wanted to see what kind it was, and if it were poisonous or not), and also unsettled to think that I had no one to kill a spider for me, like Jennifer, if I had wanted. In my own spider experiences, I recall being asleep, one night, or at least in a dozing state, and then feeling something tickling my nose, and awaking to find a nasty, garden-type crawling on my face. Of course, I was horrified and considered screaming or getting up and acting hysterical, but there was no one else around, and I was too tired, so I just brushed the spider off and went back to sleep.

I hurry around the office, checking that all the lights have been turned off. I turn off my computer and straighten my folders. The brochures had been taken down to the mailing area in plastic bins long ago. The rest of Jennifer's journals sit in a pile next to my computer, to be finished on Monday. But then I notice, to my surprise, that there is an envelope on a corner of my desk—and in the envelope, which is not marked or sealed, are two twenties and two five-dollar bills, folded together neatly. I try to remember if someone from the office had left it there for me to purchase personal supplies. There is no note with the money, and I can't recall anyone asking for anything or giving me money that afternoon. I wonder how I could have missed it—I was at my desk almost the entire day. I had left only for my half-hour lunch break, a short trip to the bathroom, and when I carried the brochures down to the mailroom around three-thirty. I check my purse, just in case, but all my own money is there. Something flashes through my mind—something Jennifer had told me about an office manager who had once worked there, Francine Dexter. I met Francine on the day she left. She had struck me as a nice, grandmotherly type. But after she was gone Jennifer told me Francine had been careless—files, letters, various office supplies had been lost or were kept in disarray. I did find some files out of order, but mostly things had been straightened out by the time I started. I don't want to leave the money on my desk, so I put the envelope in the petty cash box, in the top-left drawer of my desk. I make a mental note to ask everyone about the money on Monday. I turn out the front-room lights and lock the door.

Outside, it is a lovely evening, and I walk slowly by the Café Rafaela, festive with its strings of colored lights, music, and a lively dinner crowd. All the offices and other businesses are already closed on the street, but it's just as well, because the Café's patrons spill out onto the sidewalk, laughing and talking. I scan the restaurant and street, but I don't see Ben. He wouldn't be there, of course. There is a sign in the window that says "Help Wanted" and I think of Ben and his wistful remark about working at the Café. Maybe it wouldn't have been such a bad thing. These people look happy.

At home, I'm excited to see the next movie on my Movies-By-Mail queue has arrived—*The Pirate from*

Blackmoor. The movie is described as "visually stunning" and "bittersweet." I quickly prepare dinner—pasta and clam sauce for myself, canned liver and chicken for Cinema—and we settle down to watch the show. This is what really happens.

Set in early 1700s England, Lord Henry Dingham of Blackmoor is engaged to Lina Ogilivy, a pretty and clever stage actress, who isn't really in love with him, but wants merely to get her hands on the family fortune. Inconveniently, Henry falls in love with a beautiful American girl, Cady Griffin, who is visiting England, and he decides to dump Lina and marry Cady. Before he can propose to Cady, however, he is called away on some family trouble in Jamaica. While he is gone, Lina tells Cady Lord Henry is already engaged to her and that she, Lina, will be following him to Jamaica soon, where they will be married. Cady believes Lina (for Lina wears the ring Henry had intended for Cady) and she sails back to America, convinced Henry never loved her. Henry comes back to find Cady gone, and Lina tells him Cady hadn't wanted to marry him after all. He takes up with Lina again, and they are wed in a costly and elaborate ceremony. One day Cady, still pining over Henry, decides to sail to Jamaica, where her family owns several sugar plantations. She still believes Henry is there, and she plans to confront him. She sails to Jamaica, where she learns Lord Dingham had already returned to England and is now married to Lina. Cady decides to stick around the plantations and one of her father's plantation managers, Frederick, falls in love with her. In the meantime, Lord Dingham grows increasingly restless and more than a little tired of Lady Lina, who has gained weight and spends her time nagging and showing off their three peevish-faced children. Fed up, Lord Dingham runs away and transforms himself into the feared Pirate from Blackmoor, seizing foreign ships and giving the proceeds away to the poor. One day, he captures a particularly well-laden ship and comes face to face with a mysterious, handsome, and well-dressed man, who seems to be in charge of the ship. They fight a duel on the ship's deck, but Henry finally stabs the man when the man is momentarily distracted by a woman running up from the cabins below—the woman is Cady and the man is Frederick. She and Frederick had just wed and were sailing to Europe for their honeymoon. Cady tries to shoot Henry—she loves the good-hearted Frederick now and had long gotten over Henry—but one of Henry's pirates appears and shoots her in the heart. Lord Dingham mournfully retreats to his thousand-room mansion, to live out the rest of his days with Lady Lina and his family.

I hate the movie. Pirate Lord Henry is clearly the designated hero, but his preference for Lina over Cady, his stealing from merchants and plantation owners to toss coins to mutinous gangs of drunken sailors annoy me. I wasn't impressed by the gratuitous violence—for example, when Henry stabs Frederick and the camera zooms in on the gash and impossible amounts of spurting blood. The actress who plays Lina looks like a football player, and says over-the-top things like, "Get thy dungeons ready for the infidels!" Lord Dingham, says things to Cady, such as, "I'll love you until the day I die"—when of course, he ends up killing her husband—the one she really loves. Then, there is the ending, when Lord Dingham falls into the squishy arms of Lady Lina and moons over the greenish-faced children. I take two aspirin, and go to bed.

That night, I have a long and gloomy dream—I am waiting in deep woods at night, and an old boyfriend, Brian, shows up suddenly to comfort me, even though he has a girlfriend in my dream; he shows me a locket he wears around his neck with her name on it. I have not thought of Brian for many years, so his appearance is strange and sad. Even though he has a girlfriend, Brian stays with me, holding my hand as we find our way through the woods, but then he has to go away. Then he comes back again, because for some reason, I am still stuck in these woods alone. While I am waiting for Brian, I see something rising out of the massive black trees and into the sky— a gigantic, flashing, brilliant red and orange meteor—and I think it is wonderful; I can't wait to tell Brian about it. I wake up when Brian appears again on the path, illuminated by the meteor, flame-colored and glowing like a beating heart. I am overwhelmed with gratitude he has come back to help me.

By Monday, I have mostly forgotten *The Pirate from Blackmoor* and my strange dream, and have returned to my usual, mild-mannered weekday self. I arrive at the office early to finish Jennifer's journals, and notice something going on in one of the conference rooms. I hear voices through the door—Jennifer's and Ruth's. I catch bits of the conversation.

"— knew I needed it done—April deadline—"

Ruth said something too low for me to hear, but Jennifer's voice breaks through again.

"— problems," she says. "— know she tries. Since her grandmother died—"

I feel the blood rush to my face, but keep listening. In fact, I press my ear right up against the door. I can hear Jennifer's strong, confident voice, now only a little muffled.

"It was on her desk, before I left. Maybe she needed it for something and only meant to borrow it."

Ruth, in a calm, lower voice, says, "It could have been someone else. I wouldn't jump to conclusions—"

"I just don't think—I asked her to help me with my article last week, and she tried to put it off and blame it on those brochures. She knows how busy I am this time of the year."

I want to burst in and deny this, but remember I am not supposed to be listening. They are definitely talking about me. And yet they can't be talking about me, because I certainly don't know how busy Jennifer is. If I had been asked, I would have guessed this time of the year was among the least busy—there are no deadlines, so what is she talking about? What is it that they think I, or whoever, had needed or borrowed?

"She's very odd," says Jennifer, with an emphasis on *odd*, as if she were swallowing a mouthful of dirt. "She has no friends or family. It's a pity, with her grandmother dying last year. I can imagine all the stress she's under. It's understandable she's been seeing a therapist…"

Ruth makes some noise of surprise, but Jennifer continues, "— unstable right now. It could explain why she's taking things from the office. Poor thing. I know she's not usually like this. I feel so badly for her, but it really is affecting my work." I can imagine Jennifer shaking her head, and pressing her big-knuckled hand against her heart. I must have made a noise—a shuffle or snort or gasp—because the voices suddenly stop, and I hurry back to my desk and sit down. The conference room door opens, and I arrange my face into a neutral expression and pretend to sort through some papers.

Ruth, a petite, attractive woman in her fifties, with short pale-blond hair and black-rimmed glasses, looks tired, but she smiles at me, and nods. Jennifer stands behind her, her dark eyes large and staring, tight mouth in a straight line.

"Sarah," says Ruth, "I'm glad you're here early this

morning. Jennifer and I want to talk to you."

"Oh," I say, acting concerned. "Is something wrong?"

"Jennifer says she gave you some money on Friday to buy two tickets to the Conference luncheon this week. Do you remember that at all?"

"No, I don't," I say. "I don't remember that at all, Jennifer. I saw you on Friday afternoon, when you came back from the Educators' luncheon with Lowell. There was a lot going on in the office then, and I remember seeing you, but I don't remember you speaking to me about the tickets."

"I put the money right on your desk," she says quickly.

I feel my face grow warm. "There was some money on my desk. I didn't see it until I left that night. I put it in the petty cash box."

"I checked it," Jennifer says. "It's nearly empty. There are only a few dollar bills and some change."

"The petty cash box doesn't even have a lock," I point out. Jennifer sniffs, as if she can't believe I'm placing suspicion on everyone who has a key to the office—that would be the entire staff.

"Anybody could've taken it," I insist. "The cleaning people are here every weekend—"

At this, Jennifer looks shocked. I wonder if it's politically incorrect these days to accuse cleaning people of stealing. I never know these things, but why else would she look so indignant? Wasn't it possible?

Ruth says, "Sarah, I understand that you're having a hard time now, with a death in the family. We aren't angry with you."

"I didn't take the money. I put it in the petty cash box." And then, "I'll replace the fifty dollars. It's my fault for not putting it in a safer place."

Jennifer's face turns dark red. I can't stop staring at the brick-colored splotches on her face, because I've never seen her look so angry before. It occurs to me she actually believes I took the money. The idea is both sickening and frightening.

"I didn't take it," I say. "I put it in the box."

Ruth says, "Of course not. We believe you."

"I didn't take it!"

Jennifer says, "Sarah, we think you've been working too hard. So, we've decided to have someone help you out."

"I don't need help!"

They say some more things about "using my vacation time" and that I should "feel free to talk to them, anytime, about anything." I try to listen carefully, but all I can think of is, what am I going to do now? How could this happen? And most horrible of all—what are they going to tell Ben? I have to leave, that's all. I can't work someplace where people think I steal. I begin to feel very frantic.

"I'm fine!" I insist.

Ruth and Jennifer look at me, cautiously, as if I am some kind of dangerous animal—which only makes me feel more agitated. I want to grab Ruth's arm, and say *you've got it all wrong*, but of course, that would only make things worse. I feel extremely close to throwing a temper tantrum.

Something breaks through the wild thoughts in my head. It's Ruth's voice, saying, "So Ben will be helping out here on Tuesdays and Thursdays."

"Ben?" I say. "Here?" I look at Jennifer, but she turns away.

I stare at her, at the stolid stance and crossed arms, at the obstinate tilt of her head, at the too-straight hair. Despite the lifted chin, she doesn't look so tall now. Only heavy. Plodding. Her black clothes, I see, are outdated, and her thick shoes are stodgy. I think of Francine Dexter. I think of Brian in the woods and the gold locket. A calm begins to settle over my confused thoughts, and the rising and falling sensations begin to subside a little. Everything is happening too fast, as if the world has suddenly turned upside-down or inside-out. I have an urge to run. But I remain standing. I think about what to do.

Cracked

Helen reserved Cabin Number Thirty-Five at Greenwood National Park because it was the most affordable one-bedroom available the third week of June. They were to be in a real cabin this time, with solid walls and a locking door, and not just a wood frame covered with tarp and a zip-up door. Last summer, she and her daughters had camped out in tents, and pitched their brand-new, bright green Sundome all by themselves. Things were fine the first day, but on the second, a thunderstorm descended and transformed the tent floor into a giant waterbed—fortunately, she had enough wits about her to grab a shovel from the trunk of the car and dig an elaborate trench to drain the water away. During all this, she had instructed the twins to stay inside, a command they gladly obeyed for once. In the end, everything turned out all right. But then there were other problems. Such as bears. Bears—which admittedly they never actually ever saw—rattled the rows of metal trash bins every night, frightening Helen and keeping her awake. During one of the nights, she was sure she had seen a large shadow moving around outside the tent walls, but it could've been just another camper or the swaying trees. Helen was grateful Annie and Erin had slept soundly each night. They tried to stay awake to see the bears, but always fell asleep early and disappointingly never once heard the slightest rattle or crunch of a footstep. The summer before last they had stayed in a tent-cabin—a tarp contraption stretched over a basic frame. Their tent-cabin was nestled in the midst of fir, pine, and oak forest, surrounded by large boulders the girls could climb upon. They all had their own cots, and ate dinner every night by a bonfire. It was all very cozy, Helen not exactly charitably observed. But again, there were hassles—hiking to the shared bathroom and showers, the noise from other campers, relative lack of privacy, and again, unseen bears banging on the trash bins at night.

In spite of all this, Helen had enjoyed the trips. But this year, she decided she had had enough of bears, rainstorms, noise, and lack of sleep. Their vacation, this time, would be perfect—which meant, safer and more comfortable. They needed to be in a solid building, with four real walls, a kitchen, bathroom, beds, rugs, a door with locks, and a roof—a home away from home, as it were.

When Helen and the girls finally arrived at the Greenwood Cabins, they were pleasantly surprised to find their cabin larger than it had appeared on the website. Annie, the more adventurous of the sisters, was excited about being in a real cabin, although the building was merely a reduced bungalow—a square-shaped log structure with a wrap-around porch. Erin, more reserved and quieter, cautiously eyed the dark windows and unkempt yard of the cabin next door, which was nearly identical, except shabbier, with a scrubby yard with bare spots and patches of angry-looking weeds. As Helen and the girls unloaded the station wagon, she noticed a stocky woman with a mass of straw-colored hair, wearing baggy jeans and an oversized white T-shirt, standing with two large, sandaled feet planted on the next-door cabin's front porch. Helen guessed the woman was a local—as if she had not only lived in the woods a long, long time, but was a part of them.

Helen called out, "Hi!" A cheerful habit, she liked to think, but sometimes (such as now, upon taking a second look at the woman) she wished she had remained quiet.

The woman replied hello, but her tone was neutral, which worried Helen a bit. She hurried the children along, so they could get inside, but before they made it to the front door, the neighbor was already standing next to their station wagon and addressing Helen in a brusque and rapid monotone.

"Where you from?" she said. "Los Angeles?"

"No, San Diego."

"How long you staying? You on vacation?"

"Yes, we'll be here for just a week."

"How'd you know about this cabin?"

"On a website?"

"I know the owners of your cabin," the woman continued, nodding up and down. "Do you know them?"

"No…," Definitely something off about this person, Helen thought, but she could not figure out exactly what was wrong at the moment. The woman was a little talkative, it was true, but Helen did not want to seem unfriendly. All she could focus on now was how to get inside as quickly as possible, take a shower, and lie down for a nap. She edged away, and called out, "Have a good evening!"

The children had not even looked at the woman as they skipped inside with their luggage and bags; it seemed they had already dismissed her as someone they did not want to know. Helen, to make up for this lack of neighborliness, tried to smile at her from the porch, but she also quickly shut the door. She could see the neighbor shuffling back to her own place through the front window. Finally, Helen thought. We can start our vacation.

Inside, the furnishings were comfortable and mostly new. *All Greenwood Cabins are privately owned and reflect their owners' tastes*, the website had promised. If this was true, then the owner of this cabin was frugal and a little eccentric. There were no photos or paintings, no personal items, except a blue and white porcelain chicken perched on the kitchen counter, and a dining room chandelier made of fake—or were they real?—antlers. Annie bounced a few times on the overstuffed green-white-and-pink, floral-patterned sofa, while Erin inspected the antlers. So maybe the place was a little strange, Helen thought, even unwelcoming, perhaps. But at least the view was lovely: the living room window filled the entire front wall of the cabin, and looked out upon tall, serene pines and a quiet gravel road. Number Thirty-Five was the last house on a dead end—there was only one other house across the road, and then the one next door, belonging to the strange neighbor woman.

"Mom, look at this!" Annie shouted, as she ran from room to room, investigating closets and cabinets, pulling open drawers. Erin sat primly at the dining table, reading books she had brought with her, and apparently deciding to ignore the antlered chandelier overhead. The one room Helen definitely did not like was the bathroom, which had no windows and was paneled in redwood. The dim lighting and the excess wood created a heavy and claustrophobic effect Helen found creepy. But at least the queen bed in the one bedroom was soft and comfortable, with two flattish pillows, thin white sheets, and a navy-blue quilt. A pull-out queen sofa-bed stood by one wall, and there was another sofa-bed in the living room. As she was taking off her shoes, she happened to glance out the window next to the bed. Unfortunately, the window was covered inadequately by navy cafe curtains and possessed a perfect and undesirable view of the neighbor woman's home. Helen could still see her, standing in her yard, looking intently over at their cabin. This was a chilling sight, but Helen told herself, *she's suspicious of us. Because we're tourists. Maybe she's lonely, being out here all by herself. Poor woman.*

Helen did not feel ambitious enough to go hiking or sightseeing that day, so they stayed in and decided to take a walk later. There were plenty of other things to do, and as they had never rented a cabin before, they all agreed their novel situation was to be savored and enjoyed. Helen unpacked the cooler, threw together ham and cheese sandwiches, poured juice, and unwrapped chocolate chip cookies. Annie, munching on the cookies before Helen could tell her to eat a sandwich first, located the television's remote control, and was searching for the cartoon channel. Helen took the opportunity to set up her laptop to check her email. There was one message from Dr. Wilson, confirming her next appointment for two o'clock next Friday. Helen now had Friday afternoons off from the office—she had been promoted to manager last year, with the resultant small increase in salary and no real change in duties, but a more flexible schedule. She usually met with Dr. Wilson twice a month, for one hour each visit. Dr.

Wilson had been her therapist for the past five years. He was only a few years older than she, with a sensitive and expressive face, and straight light-brown hair that fell into his eyes. He had a gentle voice, and never accused her, either casually or accidentally, of being abnormal or crazy. Helen's parents had started that entire business—calling her crazy—while she was growing up, whenever she talked back or refused to do what they wanted. She thought she had escaped when Jim, her ex-husband, asked her to marry him, but he had merely taken over, calling her "crazy" whenever a discussion or argument did not go his way. Helen, in fact, often did feel like she was going crazy during these arguments. Jim was now married to a professor of sociology who had adopted a boy from somewhere in the Midwest. He seldom saw the twins even though he lived only two hours away. He had told her, *I'm sorry I messed up with you and the twins, but I'm making a fresh start now.* Meaning he was going to make up being a bad husband and father by being a great one for his new family. Too bad for Helen and the "old" kids.

Helen's first psychiatrist—long before Dr. Wilson, back when she was still married and living in the D.C. suburbs— had an office in Georgetown and diagnosed her as severely depressed. He put her on a medication which made her jittery, and for some reason or other she could not remember, she had simply stopped both the medication and the visits. She never heard from him again. Next was a

Yale-educated psychiatrist who diagnosed her with post-traumatic stress syndrome and put her on lithium. The lithium worked well for a few months, but then her head and hands began developing epileptic-like tremors. She stopped the lithium. Plus, she and Jim had started talking about having kids.

Two psychotherapists later, she met Dr. Wilson, and they had gotten along right away. It helped she had checked his credentials beforehand—he was a cognitive therapist, which after trial and error, she had decided was the kind she wanted to work with. She was relieved to discover Dr. Wilson's personality to be calm, good-humored, and soothing—qualities she wished she had herself. With Dr. Wilson's help, she was able to permanently stay off of medication. He, in fact, never treated her as if she was anything but a perfectly sane and normal person—flawed like everyone else, but certainly not crazy. She did not need to prove anything to Dr. Wilson, such as how she had raised her daughters and was managing her day-to-day affairs very well. She had been doing this for years, facts which seemed to have escaped the notice of her family and more disapproving friends and acquaintances.

Quite often, she had spoken of Dr. Wilson to her friend, Francine, who was also seeing a therapist. She had met Francine in high school, when they were both in the school orchestra—Helen played the violin, Francine the flute. Both were known around town for having terrible parents. Few acquaintances were interested enough to learn specifics— *strange* was the best even close friends could manage when describing the families of these two girls. Francine, however, was another who never called Helen crazy or even, quirky. After all, Francine herself had been diagnosed with depression and anxiety, and was currently on four or five different medications, some of them for physical ailments probably related to the mental ones. Francine, it was true, had a rather forbidding appearance—she was big-boned and heavy, with strawberry-blonde hair—but she was certainly not crazy. The embodiment of crazy, to Helen, was a wild-looking woman in a house-dress, shuffling around in worn slippers and talking to herself. Maybe she had seen this in a movie somewhere. The image, in any case, was not original—her own mother shuffled around in pink terry-cloth slippers, and sometimes looked quite wild and scary, but she did not talk to herself, and she did not wear house-dresses, but long skirts, sensible shoes, blouses with bow ties, colorful silk scarves, and blazers. She spent most of her time at the dining table, paying bills and doing paperwork, dusting off her houseplants, and listening to the radio— sometimes it was the classical station, sometimes talk radio, sometimes the religious channel. What Helen found most intriguing and also disturbing about her mother was how much she disliked cooking, and yet insisted on making dinner by herself every night—Helen would be assigned prep duties, but never allowed to actually cook. This antipathy came out at every meal, when the family would sit down to overcooked noodles, mushy stews, smelly cabbage soup, and so forth. No one ever called Helen's mother crazy, and Helen never thought of her that way.

Francine now lived in a small town in Illinois, and she and Helen kept in regular contact via email, phone, and holiday letters. Francine, like Dr. Wilson, had sent Helen an email the day before. Besides the usual pleasantries, gossip, and updates, Francine had raved at length over a brilliant new technique she had learned in her ceramics class. Embedded in her email was a photo of a striking royal-blue bowl, emblazoned with golden zig-zags and stripes. Helen, at first, didn't like the design, but the jagged lines on this particular bowl were bold and peculiar, and did not conform to any sort of regular pattern. She decided she did like it—better, in fact, than if it had been a plain bowl. As she read further down Francine's email, she found out why.

I broke my favorite pottery piece last week, wrote Francine, *a perfect blue bowl, which I had been working on a long time and was part of my personal collection. I was taught by my teacher, however, to repair the bowl using the process of kintsugi. This method teaches how to fix breaks with gold joinery—it does not seek to hide the scars but to make them beautiful. The breaks are now a vital part of the bowl—I won't bore you with the technicalities, but you can see here in this photo how wonderfully it works! I've learned through kintsugi that a broken bowl is no longer a damaged or second-rate work of art but a new and unique one of its own. This is now my all-time favorite piece. Do you like it?*

Helen wrote back to Francine that she did. Helen was still admiring the photo of the bowl, seeing it now from a different perspective—that it had once been broken—when she felt a sudden change in the room. Annie and Erin had stopped giggling and talking, although the television was still playing raucous cartoons.

"Mom," Annie said. "There's someone at the door."

The front door had a frosted glass window that let in the sunlight, but at this moment, the light was blocked by a shadow. It looked like a woman's shadow because of the long hair. Helen hadn't heard any noise, but apparently, Annie had seen the shadow first. The knock came a few seconds later.

"Who," she started saying, but as soon as she looked out the window, she saw that, of course, it was their neighbor. Annie and Erin ceased paying attention, and went back to their television show. Helen opened the door; the woman was holding something in her hands. Plates. Plain white dinner plates. The top one had a long brown crack down the middle.

"Hi," the woman said. "I just wanted to bring over some dishes. I thought you might need them, since sometimes they don't have all the kitchen stuff."

"Thank you," Helen said, surprised. "But I think we do have plates. The kitchen seems very well stocked actually. But it was nice of you to think of us."

The woman stood silently, still holding onto the plates. Somehow, she was right in the middle of the small living room now, instead of by the front door. How had she managed this? Helen felt confused. The woman was talking now.

"I see your internet's working," she was saying. "Mine's down. I think my phone line is not working."

"Oh, I'm so sorry to hear that."

"Actually," the woman continued, "I think the phone company made a mistake. I've been getting these huge bills, see. I think they may be accidentally charging me for your phone line."

"Did you call the phone company about that?"

The woman shrugged. "Yeah. I think they're checking into it. But if you want to know what I think," she said. "I think the owner of this cabin has it set up so's I'm getting charged for your phone line. They're always doing things like that."

"What do you mean?" Helen, asked. She felt tiny finger-like shivers crawling up her spine. "Why would they do that?"

"The owners of this here cabin, they're always causing trouble," the woman said. "Look, when I go back over to my place, I'll call the phone company again and see if they can turn my line back on. Then, can you check yours and let me know if it's still working? I just want to make sure both of our lines are working at the same time."

Helen was confused by this, but she merely said, "Okay, I'll keep an eye on it until we leave. We were going to stop by the main office for some groceries." She said this more to indicate it was time for the woman to leave, but the woman stood her ground.

"You know, that's why I wanted to know if you knew the owners of this cabin," the woman said. "they're always spying on me. Or sending people to spy on me."

"Like who?" Helen, asked. She felt rather fascinated, in spite of herself.

"Oh, there's about ten or twelve of 'em against me," the woman said, tossing her head airily. "Some of 'em are even rangers out here." She then nodded, up and down, up and down, "The people who live here are really bad. Me and my family's had trouble with them for a long time. They've even murdered one of my cousins."

At this point—later than it would've been, Helen realized, for someone who didn't have issues with what was normal or not normal—something like a neon-lighted, blinking message flashed in Helen's. Which read, *Get the hell away from this person. Now!*

"I'm very sorry about that," she said, swiftly moving towards the front door. "I'm so sorry, but we really have to go. I'll tell you if the internet is still working once we get back." She did not dare look at the children; she was afraid the panic she felt might show on her face, and she also did not want to distract the woman from leaving. Thankfully the girls were laughing at the cartoon and not paying any attention to the conversation.

The woman didn't smile and didn't move. Finally, she said, walking out the front door, still carrying her plates, "Yeah, these people are really bad."

Erin and Annie grumbled about being hustled into the car so fast, but Helen promised to buy them popsicles at the general store.

"What did that lady want?" asked Erin, in the car.

"She thought we might need some plates," Helen said.

"Oh, that was nice of her," Annie said.

"It wasn't really," Helen said, but she didn't explain herself. The girls did not quite know what to make of this, so they ignored it, as they usually did when their mother said strange things.

At the front desk, which also served as the store, Helen related the news to the manager, a tanned and unsmiling young woman wearing a name tag that read "Kymberly." She seemed to know the woman. "Oh, she musta stopped taking her meds," Kymberly said. "She's harmless."

"I don't think she's harmless," said Helen. "She was talking about someone murdering her cousins." Helen lowered her voice, "You need to move us out of that cabin right now. I'm not staying next to her."

Kymberly widened her eyes slightly and said, in a lower tone, "Oh, of course. We'll find you something closer up here."

"I don't even feel safe going back to get our things," Helen said, realizing she was beginning to think aloud, and yet unable to stop it. "But it's probably better to get it over with. So, I'll go there right now, and come back for the keys to the new cabin. If there's any problem, please send someone down right away."

As they drove back to Number Thirty-Five with their groceries, Helen informed the girls they were going to pack up as fast as possible and move to a new cabin—a bigger and better one. The manager had given them an upgrade. Annie and Erin seemed okay with this, although they were skeptical a bigger and better cabin could be possible—they were just getting used to the one they already had. But the new cabin, according to the manager, was twice as big and had three bedrooms, which meant everyone could have their own room. They drove past this new cabin along the way back—an A-frame set back from the street on a slight hill—and it did seem much larger and more luxurious. Also, it was right across the street from the main office. Helen briefly mentioned she also didn't want to be next door to that "strange" woman; she had almost said "that crazy woman." She wasn't sure yet, if the woman was really, truly, crazy. It was unnerving someone so ordinary-looking, someone who had conversed so smoothly—even if it was about spying rangers and murdered cousins—could *be* crazy. *She had looked normal*, Helen kept thinking. *She had spoken in such a normal tone of voice. No housedress or worn slippers.* Yes, the woman had seemed a little off and pushy—but then, lots of people were that way. Or were they? Helen was feeling more and more confused.

At their old cabin, she had the kids stay right near the front door, while she piled everything into the wagon, as fast as she could. She wouldn't let the kids help. The woman was not outside, but she could see a shape of a person inside the other cabin, standing at the window. Or maybe she was just imagining it?

After everything was thrown in, and the children were safely buckled into the car, she decided to go over to the woman's house one last time, pretending as if everything was okay. *I don't want her following me,* she thought, *getting mad at me for not keeping my promise*. She had promised to tell the woman the internet was working, and so that was what she would do. Helen had, in fact, checked the internet right before packing up the laptop and throwing it in her duffle bag. *I've got to keep my promises*, she thought to herself. Later, she would realize this made no sense.

The woman's porch was dark and crowded with dead or dying plants and stacks of newspapers, books, and rusting metal chairs. Through the screen door and an un-curtained window next to it, Helen could see into a cluttered dining room, dominated mostly by an enormous table covered with bills and papers. The plates the woman had brought over earlier were now piled on a sagging mustard-colored upholstered chair next to the table. Seeing this gave Helen a slight pang, and she felt a little sorry for the woman, but she told herself, "murdered cousin" and that was enough to keep her on track. She knocked firmly on the door. As she waited—and it took some time—she kept her eyes on Annie and Erin waiting in the car. She smiled and waved reassuringly. They didn't smile or wave back. *They know*, she thought, *how worried I am. How weird this is. How weird this woman and her house are. And really, what was she, Helen, doing here?* Before she could change her mind, an interior door banged shut and footsteps echoed from somewhere in the depths of the house; the woman suddenly appeared at the screen door. An awful stench began wafting out, as if some kind of strong soup had been cooking in the back kitchen for a long time. The smell was so terrible and strong Helen felt sick. It reminded her of something, but she couldn't remember what, and she didn't want to think about it. She was overwhelmed by the sole desire to get away.

"Hi!" she said, putting on a cheerful smile. "Just wanted you to know the internet's working!"

The woman stared at her suspiciously. *She never expected me to come back and tell her*, Helen thought, and her heart sank. She inched ever so slowly, backwards, down the porch stairs.

"Hope everything goes well for you," she called.

The woman continued staring after her, and then yawned and said, unperturbed, "Oh, sorry about the smell. I've been cooking…"

Helen never found out what she had been cooking. She just kept nodding, smiling, and backing away, and then, when she was at a safe distance, ran back towards the car.